Judy Moody
Predicts the Future

Megan McDonald is the award-winning author of the Judy Moody series. She says that most of Judy's stories "grew out of anecdotes about growing up with my four sisters". She confesses, "I am Judy Moody. Same-same! In my family of sisters, we're famous for exaggeration. Judy Moody is me … exaggerated." Megan McDonald lives with her husband in northern California.

You can find out more about Megan McDonald and her books at **www.meganmcdonald.net**

Peter H. Reynolds says he felt an immediate connection to Judy Moody because "having a daughter, I have witnessed first-hand the adventures of a very independent-minded girl". Peter H. Reynolds lives in Massachusetts, just down the road from his twin brother.

You can find out more about Peter H. Reynolds and his art at **www.fablevision.com**

Books by Megan McDonald
and Peter H. Reynolds

Judy Moody
Judy Moody Gets Famous!
Judy Moody Saves the World!
Judy Moody Predicts the Future
Judy Moody: The Doctor Is In!
Judy Moody Declares Independence!
Judy Moody: Around the World in 8 1/2 Days
Judy Moody Goes to College
Judy Moody, Girl Detective
Judy Moody and the NOT Bummer Summer
Judy Moody and the Bad Luck Charm
Stink: The Incredible Shrinking Kid
Stink and the Incredible Super-Galactic Jawbreaker
Stink and the World's Worst Super-Stinky Sneakers
Stink and the Great Guinea Pig Express
Stink: Solar System Superhero
Stink and the Ultimate Thumb-Wrestling Smackdown
Stink and the Midnight Zombie Walk
Stink and the Freaky Frog Freakout
Stink-O-Pedia: Super Stink-y Stuff from A to Zzzzz
Stink-O-Pedia 2: More Stink-y Stuff from A to Z
Judy Moody & Stink: The Holly Joliday
Judy Moody & Stink: The Mad, Mad, Mad,
Mad Treasure Hunt

Books by Megan McDonald

The Sisters Club
The Sisters Club: Rule of Three
The Sisters Club: Cloudy with a Chance of Boys

Books by Peter H. Reynolds

The Dot • Ish • So Few of Me
Rose's Garden • Sky Colour

Judy Moody
Predicts the Future

Megan McDonald

illustrated by
Peter H. Reynolds

WALKER
BOOKS

First published 2003 by Walker Books Ltd
87 Vauxhall Walk, London SE11 5HJ

This edition published 2011

34

Text © 2003 Megan McDonald
Illustrations © 2003 Peter H. Reynolds
Judy Moody font © 2003 Peter H. Reynolds

The right of Megan McDonald and Peter H. Reynolds to be identified as
author and illustrator respectively of this work has been asserted by them
in accordance with the Copyright, Designs and Patents Act 1988

Judy Moody ™. Judy Moody is a registered trademark
of Candlewick Press Inc., Somerville MA

This book has been typeset in Stone Informal

Printed and bound in Great Britain by Clays Ltd, St Ives plc

British Library Cataloguing in Publication Data:
a catalogue record for this book
is available from the British Library

ISBN 978-1-4063-3585-9

www.walker.co.uk

For Barbara Mauk and all the
readers of Parkview Center School
M. M.

to Dawn Haley, Master of Time & Space
P. H. R.

Table of Contents

Judy

Madame M for Moody, aka
the Sleeping Speller.

Who's

Dad

Judy's father.
Spaghetti maker and
#1 driver to Fur & Fangs.

Mum

Judy's mother.
Fond of hairbrushing to avoid
T. rex hair.

Mouse

Judy's cat.
Very predictable – or is she?

Stink

Judy's mood-ring stealing,
Virginia-creepy little brother.

Who

Rocky

Judy's baloney-eating best friend.

Ms Tater

The Crayon Lady.

Mr Todd

Judy's teacher, aka Mr New Glasses.

Frank

Mood rings don't lie. Is Judy's friend REALLY in love with her?

Jessica

Queen Bee Jessica Finch. Proud owner of Thomas Jefferson sticker. Never been to Antarctica.

The Mood Ring

Judy Moody ate one, two, three bowls of cereal. No prize. She poured four, five, six bowls of cereal. Nothing. Seven. Out fell the Mystery Prize. She ripped open the paper wrapper.

A ring! A silver ring with an oogley centre. A mood ring! And a little piece of cardboard.

WHAT MOOD ARE YOU IN? it asked.

What mood are you in?

BLACK	Grouchy. Impossible!
AMBER	Nervous. Tense
GREEN	Jealous. Envious
Blue-Green	Relaxed. Calm
DARK BLUE	Unhappy. SAD
light Blue	Happy. GLAD!
Purple	Joyful. on TOP of the World
RED	Romantic. In love!

OFFICIAL MOOD RING GUIDE
Place RING on FINGER or PRESS THUMB to CENTRE of RING hold FOR 3 SECONDS " FIND OUT WHAT MOOD you're in."

Judy slid the ring onto her finger. She pressed her thumb to the oogley centre. She squeezed her eyes tight. One one-thousand, two one-thousand, three one-thousand. She hoped the ring was purple. Purple was the best. Purple was *Joyful, On Top of the World.*

At last, she dared to look. Oh no! She couldn't believe her eyes. The ring was black. She knew what black meant, even without the directions. Black said *Grouchy, Impossible*. Black was for a bad, mad mood!

Maybe I counted wrong, thought Judy. She closed her eyes and pressed the ring again. She thought only good thoughts this time. Happy thoughts.

She thought about the time she and Rocky and Frank put a fake hand in the toilet to play a trick on Stink. She thought about the time she got a picture of her elbow in the newspaper. She thought about the time Class 3T collected enough bottles to plant trees in the rainforest. She thought of purple things. Socks and rocks and Popsicles.

Judy Moody opened her eyes.

She flunked! The ring was still black.

Could the mood ring be wrong? Judy did not think rings could lie. Especially rings with directions.

Judy froze her thumb on an ice cube and pressed the ring's centre. Black.

She ran her thumb under hot water and pressed it again. Black, black, blacker than black. Not one teeny bit purple.

I guess I'm in a bad mood and don't even know it, thought Judy. What could I be mad about?

Judy Moody went looking for a bad mood.

She found her dad outside, planting fall flower bulbs.

"Dad," she said, "will you take me to Fur & Fangs?"

Judy hated when her dad was too busy to take her to the pet store. She could already feel the bad mood coming on.

"Sure," said Dad. "Just let me rinse my hands."

"Really?" asked Judy.

"Really."

"But you look really busy. And I have homework."

"It's OK," said Dad. "I'm about finished. I'll just wash my hands and we'll go."

"But what about my homework?"

"Do it after dinner," said Dad.

"Never mind," said Judy.

"Huh?" asked her dad.

Judy Moody went looking for an even better bad mood.

It really bugged her when her mum told her to brush her hair. So Judy took out her ponytails on purpose. Her hair stuck out in *T. rex* spikes. Her bangs fell over her eyes.

She found her mum reading in the pink chair.

"Hi, Mum."

Her mum smiled at her. "Hi, honey."

"Aren't you going to say anything?" Judy asked.

"Like what?"

"Like, 'Go brush your hair. Get your hair out of your eyes. Your hair looks like a *T. rex.*' Anything."

"It's from the ponytails, honey. It'll be fine after you wash it tonight."

"But what if somebody came to our house and knocked on the door right this very second?" Judy asked.

"Like who? Rocky?" asked Mum.

"No, like the president of the United States," Judy said.

"Tell the president you'll be right down. Then run upstairs and brush your hair."

It was no use. Judy Moody had to find Stink. If anybody could put her in a bad mood, Stink could. The baddest.

Upstairs, Judy barged right into Stink's room without knocking.

"Stink! Where's all my doctor stuff?"

"What doctor stuff? I don't have any."

"But you always have my doctor stuff."

"You told me to stop taking everything."

"Do you have to listen to everything I say?" asked Judy.

Judy glared at her ring. "This mood ring lies." She yanked it off and threw it into the trash.

Stink fished the ring out of the trash. "A mood ring? Cool!" He tried on the ring. It turned black. Bat-wing black.

"See?" said Judy. "Worthless!"

Stink pressed his thumb to the oogley

centre. The ring turned green! Green as a turtle's neck. Green as a toad's belly.

Judy could not believe her eyes. "Let me see that," she said. It was green all right. "Stink, you can give me back my mood ring now."

"You threw it in the trash," Stink told her, waving his mood-ring hand in front of her. "It's mine now."

"Yuck! Green looks like pond scum."

"Does not!"

"Green means jealous. Green means green with envy. Green means you wish you were me."

"Why would I wish that? You don't have a mood ring," said Stink.

"C'mon, Stinker. I went through seven bowls of cereal for that ring. I gave up going to Fur & Fangs for that ring. I froze and burned myself for that ring."

"It's still mine," said Stink.

"ROAR!" said Judy.

Eeny Meany Green Zucchini

The next day, Judy was in a mood. The burnt-toast kind of bad mood. The kind that turns your mood ring B-L-A-C-K.

If only she could convince Stink that she had magic powers. A person with magic powers should own a mood ring. What good was a mood ring in the hands of someone with un-magic powers?

Where was that Stink-a-Roo anyway?

Probably down in the living-room reading the encyclopedia.

Judy ran downstairs. Stink was lying on the floor with encyclopedias all around him, wiggling his loose tooth.

"I knew it!" said Judy. "I just predicted you'd be reading the encyclopedia. I have special powers, super-duper magic powers, see-the-future powers!"

"I'm always reading the encyclopedia," said Stink. "Which letter am I on?"

"*M,*" said Judy.

"WRONG!" said Stink. "*S!*"

"I still predicted it," said Judy. What else could she predict?

Judy went to the kitchen and brought back a Tasty Tuna Treat for Mouse.

She hid it in her pocket.

"I predict that Mouse will come into the room," she said. She waved the Tasty Tuna Treat behind her back, where Stink couldn't see it.

Mouse came slinking into the room. "Mouse!" said Judy. "What a surprise! Except … I predicted it! Ha!"

"Mouse always comes into the room we're in," said Stink.

"Well, what if I said I could read our mother's mind?"

"I'd rather read the encyclopedia," said Stink.

"Stink, you have to come with me!" said Judy. "So I can prove my amazing powers of prediction!" Stink followed Judy into Mum's office.

"Hi, Mum," said Judy. "Guess what?"

"What is it?" said Mum, looking up over her glasses.

"I know what you're thinking," said Judy. She squeezed her eyes shut, wrinkled her nose, and pressed her fingertips to her temples.

"You're thinking ... you wish I'd clean under my bed for once instead of bugging you. You're thinking ... you wish Stink would get his homework out of the way for the weekend."

"Amazing! That's exactly what I'm thinking!" said Mum.

"See?" said Judy.

"Were you really thinking that, Mum?" asked Stink.

"Now I predict that Dad will walk into the house," said Judy.

"You heard the garage door," said Stink.

"True. OK, it's Dad's night to cook. I predict spaghetti."

"All he knows how to make is either spaghetti or ziti."

Stink ran into the kitchen. Judy ran after him.

"Dad, Dad!" Stink said. "What's for dinner?"

"Spaghetti," said Dad.

"Lucky guess," Stink said to Judy.

"ESP," Judy said.

"OK," said Stink. "I'm thinking of a number."

"It doesn't work like that," said Judy.

"C'mon! What's the number?"

Judy grabbed a dish towel and wrapped it around her head like a turban.

She closed her eyes. She pressed her fingertips to her temples. She made funny noises. "Ali Baba, abracadabra. Eeny meany green zucchini."

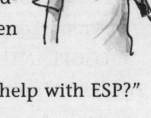

"Does the dish towel help with ESP?" asked Stink.

"Quiet! I'm concentrating."

"Hurry up. What am I thinking?"

"You're thinking I don't really have Extra Special Powers."

"Right," said Stink.

"You're thinking ESP shouldn't take this long," Judy said.

"Right! What about my number?"

Stink's favourite number was always his age. "Seven," said Judy.

"Right again!" said Stink. "Now I'm thinking of a colour."

"Pond-scum green?" said Judy.

"Wrong! Eggplant," said Stink.

"EGGPLANT! Eggplant is not a colour! Eggplant is not even an egg. Eggplant is a vegetable. A squeegy-weegy vegetable."

"I was still thinking it," said Stink. "You

have about as much magic power as an eggplant. A squeegy-weegy eggplant."

"Face it, Stink. I have special powers. Even without my mood ring."

"So you don't need it back," said Stink, flashing the ring under Judy's nose.

"A person with special powers, such as mine, should have a mood ring. It goes with predicting the future, like a crystal ball. Has the ring turned purple on you?"

"Nope."

"See? It only turns purple on Extra-Special-Powers people. It turns pond-scum green on plain old encyclopedia readers."

Stink stared at the ring.

"In fact, I predict that your finger will

turn green and fall off if you don't give me back my ring," said Judy.

"I'm never taking it off," said Stink.

"We'll see," said Judy.

Toady Calling

On Saturday, Stink was reading the encyclopedia. Again! He wiggled his loose tooth some more. With his mood-ring finger, of course. The mood ring glowed. It glittered. It gleamed. Stink scratched his head with his mood-ring finger about one hundred times a minute.

"Stink, do you have lice or something?" Judy asked.

"No," said Stink. "I have a mood ring!" He laughed himself silly.

Mr Lice Head was giving Judy a bad case of the Moody blues. She could not stay in the same room and watch her mood-ring-that-wasn't-hers one more minute. She needed to think.

Judy looked out the back door. It was raining outside. She pulled on her rubber boots, dashed across the backyard and crawled inside the Toad Pee Club Clubhouse (aka the old blue tent).

Plip-plop, plip-plop went the rain. It was lonely in the clubhouse all by herself. She wished the other members of the Toad Pee Club were here. Well, at least Rocky and Frank Pearl, not Stink.

She even missed Toady. Maybe she shouldn't have let Toady go after all. Even if it was to help save the world.

Ra-reek! Ra-reek! went the toads outside.

Boing! Just like that, Judy had an idea. A perfect predicts-the-future idea.

She, Judy Moody, predicted Stink would give the mood ring back in no time. All she needed was a yogurt container, a little luck and a toad.

☙   ☙   ☙

Judy held out her umbrella and bent over, searching for toads. She looked in a pile of logs. She looked inside a loop of garden hose. She looked under the old bathtub behind the shed.

Ra-reek! Ra-reek!

She could hear about a thousand toads, but couldn't see a single one. There had to be a Toady-looking toad around here somewhere. It's not like she was looking for a rare north-east beach tiger beetle or anything.

Judy was just about to give up and go back inside when she heard something. Something close. Something right there on the back porch. Something like *Ra-reek! Ra-reek!*

It was Mouse! Mouse sounded like a toad!

The cat was drinking from her water dish.

Wait! Mouse did not sound like a toad. Mouse's water dish sounded like a toad. A real live toad was swimming in Mouse's water dish!

Judy took a deep breath. Slowly, slowly, she held out the yogurt container.

"Ha!" Judy trapped the toad under the yogurt container. She wondered if it looked like Toady. She lifted up the container to study the toad.

RA-REEK! Boing!

The toad hopped across the porch, down the steps and into the wet grass.

"Here, Toady, Toady. Nice toad. Pretty boy. Come to Judy."

Ra-reek! Ra-reek! "Gotcha!" This time Judy caught him with her hands.

He was the same size as Toady. He had speckles and warts and bumps like Toady. He even had a white stripe down his back. Just like Toady.

"Same-same!" said Judy.

All of a sudden, Judy felt something warm and wet on her hand.

"Toady Two!" she cried.

☙ ☙ ☙

Sneaky Judy hid Toady Two under a bucket in the tent. Then she went to find Stink.

"Hey, Stink," yelled Judy, dripping in the doorway. "Let's go hunt for stuff in the backyard." Stink did not even look up from reading the *S* encyclopedia.

"*S* is for *Saturday*," said Judy. "*S* is for *Stand Up! S* is for I'm going to *Scream* if you don't come outside."

Stink flipped a page.

"Are you coming, or are you just going to sit there?" she asked.

"Sit there," said Stink.

Judy tapped her feet. She tap-tap-tapped her fingers.

"*S* is for *Shh!*" said Stink. "I'm reading about a lizard with a tail that turns blue. A skink."

"Skinks stink," said Judy. Stink ignored her.

She, Judy Moody, liked those blue-tailed skinks as much as the next person. But she was not in an *S*-is-for-*Sitting-Still* mood. She had to get Stink outside. Fast!

"I've seen a stinky skink before."

"Where?" asked Stink.

"The backyard. C'mon, Stinker. We can look for skinks!" said Judy.

"You think?" asked Stink. He closed the encyclopedia.

"Rain is perfect skink-hunting weather!" said Judy.

Stink looked for skinks in the cracks on the back porch. He looked in the flowerpot. He looked under Mouse's dish.

"What makes you think we can find a skink anyway?" asked Stink.

"ESP. Extra-special Skink Powers. Keep looking."

"I'm looking, I'm looking."

"Whoever finds a skink first gets an ice cream at Screamin' Mimi's. Wait. What's that?"

Judy closed her eyes. "Humm, baba,

humm. Nee nee nee nee nee. Ohmmmm.
I feel a presence."

"A skink?"

"I hear … a sound."

"Is it a skink or something?" asked Stink.

"Or something," said Judy. She closed
her eyes again. She pressed her fingers to
her forehead. "Yes! I'm getting a colour.
Greenish brown."

"Everything in the backyard is greenish
brown."

"I see bumps. It's bumpy," said Judy.

"Skinks are not bumpy," said Stink.

"Definitely bumpy," said Judy.

"Is it bumpy like dead leaves? Skinks
love dead leaves," said Stink.

"Bumpy like warts," said Judy. "Now I see something to do with water."

Stink looked around. "It's raining. Water is everywhere."

"I said something *to do* with water," said Judy. *Bucket. Bucket.* She tried hard to send Stink an ESP, but he wasn't getting the message.

"Wait! The presence is saying something," said Judy. "Yes. It's speaking to me. Ra-reek! Ra-reek!"

"A toad?" asked Stink. "Is the presence a toad?"

"Yes," said Judy. "No. Wait. Yes!"

"A toad? For real? Toady?" asked Stink. "Is it Toady calling?"

"YES!" said Judy. "It's Toady. Toady is calling to me. RARE!"

"Where? Where is he?" asked Stink.

"Wait. No. Sorry. I had it. But I'm losing it now."

"NO!" cried Stink. "Close your eyes again. Concentrate. Feel the presence or something."

"Do it with me," said Judy. Stink and Judy held hands. They closed their eyes. "Say *eeny meany green zucchini,*" said Judy.

"Eeny greeny mean zucchini."

"Yes! I see it! I see a bucket. And I see something blue. A blue roof? No. It's a tent. Yes. A blue tent!"

Stink raced inside the tent and went straight for the bucket. He lifted it up.

Ra-reek!

"Toady Two!" said Judy.

"Toady Two?"

"I mean Toady, T-O-O. As in *also*. As in not just some crummy old bucket."

"Toady! You're back!" cried Stink. He hugged the toad in his hands. He grinned a loose-tooth grin. "I missed you. You came back. For real. Just like Judy said."

"Like I predicted," said Judy. "Just call me Madame Moody. Madame M for short."

"Is it really him?" said Stink.

"Who else?"

"Toady, I didn't let you go. Judy did. Honest. Don't ever leave again."

Stink held Toady in both hands. "I don't even care if he makes me a member of the

Toad Pee Club again," said Stink.

"Ick," said Judy.

Stink kissed Toady on his beady-eyed, bumpy little head.

"Now can I have my ring back?" she asked.

Madame M for Moody

Judy and Stink came in out of the rain. They ate Fig Newtons and sipped hot chocolate with fancy straws.

"You really are psychic," said Stink.

"Told you," said Judy. She chomped on her cookie.

"I thought it was just another one of your tricks," said Stink.

"Uh-uh." *Chomp, chomp.*

"Toady came back. And you knew. You predicted it."

"Uh-huh."

"At first I didn't believe you," said Stink. "But then I saw the little black stripe."

Judy's Fig almost fell out of her Newton. "What little black stripe?"

"The little black stripe over Toady's right eye. No other toads have it. Just Toady. That's how I knew it was him."

"Let me see that toad," said Judy.

Stink took Toady out of the yogurt container. Doctor Judy Moody examined the toad like she was giving a check-up. Stink was right. He did have a little black stripe, just like Toady. Could it be?

She, Judy Moody, predicted that Toady came back, and ... he did?

"You can have your mood ring back," said Stink.

"Huh?"

"Your mood ring?" said Stink. "You were right. It really does belong to a person with super-duper special powers. Here. Take it." Stink wiggled the ring, but it was stuck.

"*S* is for *Stuck!*" said Stink. He held out his hand. "I can't get it off! Ack!! My finger! It's green!"

"Stink, it's OK."

"But you predicted my finger would turn green and fall off. Look! Now it *is* green! Hurry up. Before my finger falls off."

"*S* is for *Soap*," said Judy.

Judy took Stink over to the sink and soaped up his finger. She twirled the ring. She twisted the ring. She pulled the ring. She yanked the ring. *POP!*

"Mine at last," said Madame *M*-for-*Moody* Judy.

On Monday morning, Judy Moody woke up early. What might have been a blucky old maths-test Monday did not seem blucky one bit.

She did not put on her tiger-striped pyjamas for school. She did not put on her I ATE A SHARK T-shirt. She put on her best-mood-ever clothes – purple-striped pants, a not-itchy fuzzy green sweater with a star, and Screamin' Mimi's ice-cream-cone socks. And her mood ring.

Light blue! Light blue was the next best thing to purple. Light blue meant *Happy, Glad*. She was glad to have her ring back. She was happy with the world.

"Purr-fect!" she said to Mouse. Mouse rubbed up against her leg.

On the bus, she told good-mood jokes. "Why did the third grader eat so many cornflakes?" Judy asked her friend Rocky.

"I don't know. Because all the snowflakes were melted?" asked Rocky.

"No!" said Judy. "To get a mood ring!" Judy cracked herself up.

She told jokes all the way to school. Stink plugged his ears. Rocky just shuffled his deck of magic cards.

"You're not laughing at my jokes," Judy complained.

"Um, I'm worried about Mr Todd's maths test," said Rocky. "Fractions!"

Normally Judy would have worried too. Not today. Her mood ring had just turned blue-green for *Relaxed, Calm.*

☙   ☙   ☙

"OK, class," said Mr Todd. "A new week. I know we have a few tests this week. Maths test today. Spelling test tomorrow. But don't forget, we have a special visitor next week. Monday. One week from today. A real live author! She's also an artist. She wrote and illustrated a book about crayons."

"A baby book?" asked Rocky.

"I think you'll find it interesting," said Mr Todd. "There's so much to know about crayons." Mr Todd grinned. Since when did crayons make her teacher so happy?

In Reading, Mr Todd read *The Case of the Red-eyed Mummy*. Judy solved it before anyone else did. When it came time to write a mystery in her journal, Judy wrote *The Mystery of the Missing Mood Ring*, in which she, Judy Moody, solved the case.

All morning, Judy raised her mood-ring hand, even when she didn't know the answer.

Even Mr Todd noticed the ring. "What's that you've got there?" he asked Judy.

"A mood ring," Judy said. "It predicts stuff. Like what mood you're in."

"Very nice," said Mr Todd. "Let's hope everybody's in the

mood for the maths test. Class 3T, put all books away, please."

Judy leaned over and asked her friend Frank Pearl if he had studied his fractions.

"Yep," said Frank. "But I'll be half happy and half glad when it's over."

Judy looked over her shoulder at Jessica Finch. She looked *Relaxed, Calm.* Jessica Finch probably ate fractions for breakfast: 1/4 glass of orange juice, 1/2 piece of toast, 3/4 jar of strawberry jam!

Judy took her time on the test. She did not bite off her Grouchy pencil eraser. She did not make grouchy faces at the maths test. She was even *Relaxed, Calm* about making up a word problem.

A rainbow has seven colours (ROY G. BiV)

Problem

A rainbow has seven colours (ROY G. BiV)
If Judy has a purple mood ring, Rocky
has a blue mood ring, Frank has a
red mood ring and Stink has a green
mood ring, how much of the rainbow
do they have? (Answer has to be a
fraction!)

Hint: There are four mood rings, or four
out of seven colours of the rainbow.

ANSWER: 4/7!

☺ ☺ ☺

At recess, everybody crowded around Judy.

"Where'd you get that mood ring?"

"Ooh, let me try!"

Time to daze and amaze her friends.

"Who wants to go first?" asked Judy.

"Me me me me me!" Everybody pushed and shoved and begged.

"Wait," said Judy. "Before anyone puts the ring on, I'm going to make a prediction."

Judy looked at the chart that came with the mood ring. Amber meant *Nervous, Tense*. Rocky was nervous about the maths test.

"Madame M predicts the ring will turn amber on Rocky," said Judy. Rocky slid the ring onto his finger. It turned black.

"Madame M is W-R-O-N-G!" said Rocky.

"Just wait!" Judy said. "The mood ring doesn't lie." Everybody crowded around Rocky to watch. Slowly, it did turn amber, just like Judy said!

"How did you know?" asked Rocky.

"Madame M knows all," said Judy. "I predict it will be light blue on Frank. I can feel it," said Judy.

"Is blue sad?" asked Frank. "Because I don't feel sad. And I don't want to think of sad things. Like the time I didn't have a club for my Me collage and the time I was a human centipede and somebody broke my finger."

"Boo-hoo. *Dark* blue is *Unhappy, Sad.* C'mon, just try the ring on!"

Frank slipped the ring onto his finger.

Judy crossed her fingers and whispered to herself, "Light blue, light blue, light blue." Not a minute later the ring turned light blue.

"Same-same!" said Judy. "Light blue is *Happy, Glad*. That's the colour it turned on me, too."

"Ooh-ooh! Frank got the same colour as Judy!"

"Frank Pearl and Judy are in love!" everybody teased.

"Frank Pearl's getting married. To Judy Moody! And he already has the ring!"

Frank turned bright red. He practically threw the ring at Jessica Finch.

"I hope it's pink on me," said Jessica.

"There is no pink," said Judy. "But there's GREEN," she said loudly to the ring.

Before Jessica could try the ring on, the bell rang and recess was over.

  ⟨ ⟨ ⟨

In Science, Mr Todd was talking about weather and the world's temperature rising. Judy sharpened her pencil with her mood-ring hand. She threw trash in the trash can with her mood-ring hand. She passed a note to Frank with her mood-ring hand.

Judy did not see Mr Todd's temperature rising!

"I wish I had a mood ring," whispered Jessica Finch.

"You have to eat a lot of cereal," Judy whispered back, a little too loudly.

"Judy, is there a problem?" asked Mr Todd.

"No," said Judy, sitting on her hands.

As soon as Mr Todd turned back to the board, Judy played with her ring to make Jessica jealous. She twisted the ring. She twirled the ring. She spun the ring on her finger. It flew off, hit Mr Todd's desk, and landed at Mr Todd's feet.

Mr Todd bent over and picked it up. "Judy," he said, "I'm afraid I'll have to keep the ring for you until the end of the day."

Judy turned one, two, three shades of red. Even Madame M had not predicted the mood ring would get her into trouble.

Mr Todd slipped the ring onto the top of his index finger. He opened his desk drawer. As he put it away, Judy thought she caught a glimpse of colour.

Could it be? No. Wait. Maybe. It was! YES! Judy was 3/4 sure. She was 9/10 sure. Mr Todd might have the ring, but she, Judy Moody, had seen red. Red as in Red Hots. Red as in ruby slippers.

RARE squared!

The Sleeping Speller

That night, Judy met Frank at the library to study for the spelling test.

"Hey! You got your mood ring back from Mr Todd," said Frank when Judy arrived.

"Yes!" said Judy, holding up her hand to admire it. She would never, ever, not ever take her mood ring off again until it turned positively purple. Except at school, of course. Mr Todd said no more mood rings at school. While she was at school, she would be sure to keep it safe. Hidden in her extra-special baby-tooth box.

"Speaking of Mr Todd, have you seen the spelling words?" asked Frank. "They are hard, as in D-I-F-F-I-C-U-L-T!"

Judy looked at the list. "*Woodbine!* What in the world's a woodbine?"

"Who knows?" asked Frank.

Frank went to get the big dictionary. He came back carrying it like it weighed a hundred pounds. They opened it on the table.

"*'Woodbine,'*" Judy read out loud. "'A vine that wraps around trees.'"

"'Also called Virginia creeper,'" read Frank.

"RARE!" said Judy.

"Creepy!" said Frank.

"I'm tired of studying," said Judy.

"Tired?! We only learned one word!" said Frank.

"Let's look at books," said Judy.

Frank followed Judy down a long row of high shelves. "Ooh. What books are these? It's all dark and dusty."

"I hope there aren't any Virginia-creepy vines around here," said Judy in a spooky voice.

Frank found a book with pictures of bones and the creepy insides of stuff. "Body parts!" he said.

Judy went to find the librarian.

"What did you get?" Frank asked when she came back.

"Predict Your Head Off!" said Judy. "It's all about people who predicted stuff about the future. Lynn helped me find it. She's the cool librarian with the fork-and-pie earrings. Not the mad-face librarian."

"Hey! It's a Big Head book. I love those. How come they draw the people with such big heads, anyway?" Frank asked.

"Maybe it's to hold all those big ideas about the future. Look, see?" said Judy, pointing to her book. "These people predicted earthquakes and fires and babies being born."

"Nobody can predict the future," said Frank. "Can they?"

"Ya-huh!" said Judy. "It says right here. Books don't lie."

"Let me see," said Frank.

"See? Jeane Dixon, Famous American Fortune-teller. She was some lady in Washington, DC, who stared into her eggs one morning and predicted that President Kennedy would be shot. And she predicted an earthquake in Alaska."

"It also says she predicted that Martians would come to Earth and take away teenagers. I wish that would happen to my big sister."

"If only Stink were a teenager," said Judy.

"Look! It says here that that Jeane Dixon lady saw stuff in whipped cream!" said Frank.

"I've seen stuff in whipped cream too," said Judy. "Lots of times."

"Like what?"

"Like chocolate sprinkles," Judy said, and they both cracked up.

"Hey, look at this," said Judy. "This book can help us with our spelling test. For real."

"No way."

"Way! See this guy?"

"The bald guy with the bow tie?"

"Yep. It says that he lived right here in Virginia. They called him the Sleeping Prophet. When he was our age, like a hundred years ago, he got into trouble in school for being a bad speller. One night he fell asleep with his spelling book under his head. When he woke up, he knew every word in the book. RARE!"

"I'm still going to study," said Frank.

"Not me!" said Judy, wriggling into her coat.

"What are you going to do?" asked Frank.

"I'm going to go home and sleep," said Judy.

❂   ❂   ❂

When Judy got home, Stink was at the door.

"I don't have to study for my spelling test," she said, and gave him a big fat hug.

"What's that for?" asked Stink.

"That's for just because."

"Just because why?"

"Just because tomorrow I am going to know tons and tons of words, like *woodbine*."

"Wood what?"

"It's a creepy vine. It wraps around trees."

"So go find a tree to hug," said Stink.

Instead, Judy went to find the dictionary. The fattest dictionary in the Moody house. She took it from her mum's office and lugged it up to her room. She did not open it up. She did not look inside. She put the big red dictionary under her pillow. Then she got into her cosy bowling-ball

pyjamas. She pretended the bowling balls were crystal balls. When she brushed her teeth, she thought she saw a letter in her toothpaste spit. *D* for *Dictionary*.

Judy climbed under the covers and leaned back on her pillow. Youch! Too hard. She got two more pillows. At last, she was ready to dream.

Even before she fell asleep, she dreamed of being Queen of the Spelling Bee, just like Jessica Finch was one time for the whole state of Virginia. She dreamed of Mr Todd's smiling face when he passed back the tests. Most of all, she dreamed of getting 110% – zero-wrong-plus-extra-credit – on her spelling test.

She could hardly wait for school tomor-row. For once, she, Judy Moody, not Jessica (Flunk) Finch, would get a Thomas Jeffer-son tricorn-hat sticker for *Great job, good thinking.*

ZZZZZZZZZZzzzzzzz...

Preposterous Hippopotamus

When Judy woke up the next morning, her neck was so stiff she felt like a crookneck squash. But her head did not feel the least bit bigger. It did not even feel heavy from carrying around so many new words. She looked in the mirror. Same Judy-head as always.

At breakfast, Judy stared into her eggs, just like Jeane Dixon, Famous American

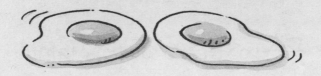

Fortune-teller. She thought she felt an earthquake! The earthquake was Stink, shaking the ketchup bottle onto his eggs.

"Stink, that's *preposterous*!" said Judy.

"What's that mean?" asked Stink.

"It means *ridiculous*," said Judy.

"Like funny or silly," said Mum.

"Think *hippopotamus*," said Judy.

RARE! The dictionary-under-the-pillow thing really worked! Big words were flying out of her mouth faster than spit.

Judy was in a positively purple, On-Top-of-Spaghetti-and-the-World mood. She wished she could take her mood ring to school. If only.

On the bus, Judy told Rocky that his new magic trick was *bewildering*.

At school, Frank gave Judy a miniature hotel soap from his collection. "I already have this one," he said. Judy told him his treat was very *unexpected*.

Then she asked Jessica (Flunk) Finch if she looked forward to the spelling test with *anticipation*.

"Why are you talking funny?" asked Jessica.

Mr Todd passed out lined paper for the test. He told the class, "Only four more school days until our special visitor comes to class."

Something was not the same. Something was different. Something was *peculiar, unusual.* Mr Todd had new glasses! And he was wearing a tie. A crayon tie! Mr Todd had never dressed up for a spelling test before.

"Your new glasses are very *noticeable*," said Judy.

"Thank you, Judy," said Mr Todd with a goofy grin.

During the test, Judy Moody's Grouchy pencil flew across the page like never before. She spelled *alfalfa* and *apple sauce*. She spelled *cobweb* and *crystal*. She hardly even had to erase, except on *zucchini*.

And she used the extra-credit word in a sentence! *Crayon.* What kind of a bonus word was *crayon*? Mr Todd had crayons on the brain. For sure and absolute positive.

Madame M predicts that the Crayon Lady will soon come to Class 3T to see Mr Todd's crayon tie.

Judy's extra-credit word sentence was practically a paragraph! And she used the bonus word twice! Double R-A-R-E!

Judy was the first one to finish, even before the Queen Bee Speller Jessica Finch. Jessica wasn't even using her lucky pencil! What was that girl thinking?

⊚   ⊚   ⊚

At the lunch table, she, Judy Moody, was in a predict-the-future mood.

"Don't open your lunches yet," Judy

said to everybody. "Madame M will predict what's inside."

"Hurry up," said Rocky. "I'm hungry."

Judy shut her eyes. This was so easy. "I see baloney. Baloney sandwiches." Rocky, Frank and Jessica each held up a baloney sandwich.

Everyone was amazed.

Now the moment she'd been waiting for. "I have another prediction," said Judy in a loud voice. "One about tomorrow. Something big. Something that's never happened in Class 3T before."

"Really? Tell us! What?"

"I, Judy Moody, will get zero-wrong-plus-extra-credit on the spelling test! 110%! Pass it on."

"That's as preposterous as a H-I-P-P-O-P-O-T-A-M-U-S," Jessica said.

"You didn't even study," Frank said.

"You never even got 100% in Spelling," said Rocky.

"Thanks a lot," said Judy. What a bunch of baloney eaters. "That was before I became the Sleeping Speller, before I learned about sleeping with the dictionary under my pillow."

"But Mr Todd didn't pass our tests back yet," said Frank. "You don't even know if it really worked."

Judy rolled her eyeballs around. She made thinking noises. "Humm, baba, humm. Mr Todd is correcting the papers right now. I see a Thomas Jefferson sticker.

A tricorn hat. For *Great job, good thinking.*"

"You're 110% cuckoo," Rocky told Judy.

"Just call me the Sleeping Speller," Judy said.

Antarctica

Judy predicted it would be hard to sit still until Mr Todd passed back the spelling tests. She predicted right. She felt antsy as an anthill. Jumpy as a jumping bean.

At last, the time came.

"Good work. Keep it up," Mr Todd was saying as he walked around the room, passing back tests and handing out cookies. Heart-shaped cookies. With sprinkles!

And he was humming. Mr Todd never hummed! And he never brought heart-shaped cookies with sprinkles. Not even on Valentine's Day, which it wasn't.

It had to be a sign. A sign that she, the Sleeping Speller, had done super-duper *stupendous* on her spelling test. That would definitely put Mr Todd in a good mood.

In less than one minute, Class 3T would see that she, Madame M, had ESP. Extra-special Spelling Powers. Just like Jeane Dixon, Famous American Fortune-teller. And Sleeping Speller Man.

In less than one minute, Judy had her test back. And the only cookie left was a broken heart.

Dear Mr President! Something was not right! Her paper did not have a Thomas Jefferson sticker. It did not even have a president. Or a sticker. It had a feather. A musty, dusty-looking, old-timey rubber-stamp feather. A quill pen. A quill pen meant *Keep trying*. A quill pen meant *You have more work to do*. A quill pen was as *preposterous* as a *hippopotamus*.

At the bottom of her test was a note from Mr Todd. It said, "*Tortilla* has two *l*'s. *Zigzag* is one word."

Judy didn't see why *tor-tee-yah* had any *l*'s at all. And *zig* and *zag* sure seemed like two words to her. Who wrote the dictionary anyway? Mrs Merriam and Mr Webster were going to hear from her.

All eyes were on Judy. She turned fire-engine red. Hide-your-face-in-your-hands red. Big-fat-dictionary red.

The Sleeping Speller was a flop. The Sleeping Speller was a flubber-upper. The Sleeping Speller was a big fat phoney-baloney.

Maybe Jessica (Flunk) Finch got a musty, dusty quill pen too! Judy knew it was a bad-mood thought. Judy knew she was supposed to keep her eyes on her own paper. But she couldn't help herself. She turned around.

Jessica Finch beamed. Jessica Finch gleamed. Like the day she was crowned Queen Bee and got her picture in the paper. Jessica Finch sat up straight and

proud as a president. She held up her paper for Judy to see.

"I knew it!" Jessica said. "I got a Thomas Jefferson tricorn hat!"

A tricorn hat did not mean *flubber-upper*. A tricorn hat did not mean *Better luck next time. Keep trying. You need more practice!* A tricorn hat meant *Hats off to you!*

"How did you know?" Judy asked. Judy was supposed to be the one predicting the future, not Jessica Finch.

"I used my brain," said Jessica. "Some people studied."

Judy was green with *Jealous, Envious.* And she did not need her mood ring to prove it.

The class buzzed. They turned on Judy like a pack of stinging bees.

"Hey, what happened to the Sleeping Speller?"

"The Sleeping Speller fell asleep!"

Judy Moody gave them all a Virginia-creeper stare.

"Hold on, everybody," said Mr Todd-the-Hummer. "You know that in this class we keep our eyes on our own papers."

"But Mr Todd, Judy Moody *said*. She told us. She predicted she would get a 110% perfect paper. She predicted WRONG!"

"Nobody can really predict the future!" said Rocky. "Right, Mr Todd?"

"Well, we all play a part in creating our own futures," said Mr Todd. "So, in the future, I hope you'll concern yourselves with your own work, not the work of the person next to you."

That got everybody quiet.

"Now. Let's move on to ... Science. Take out your Weather Notebooks."

Judy did not take out her Weather Notebook. She was comparing her paper to Jessica Finch's.

"Judy," said Mr Todd, "I'm afraid you haven't heard a word I've said. I'm going to have to ask you to go to Antarctica."

Antarctica!

Antarctica was a desk at the back of the room with a map on top. A map with a lot of icebergs and a lot of penguins. And a sign that said CHILL OUT. The sign might as well have said IN BIG TROUBLE.

Judy looked at Mr Todd. He did not look one bit like the Hummer, Mr New Glasses, Mr Crayon Tie, the teacher who brought heart-shaped cookies to class. He looked like Mr Toad.

Judy hung her head and walked to the desk at the back of the room. Jessica Finch

was Thomas Jefferson. And she, Judy Moody, was president of Antarctica.

Judy was mad enough to spit. How could Madame M ever predict the future if she could not even predict one lousy spelling test?

One thing she could predict was the weather. It was cold in Antarctica. Cold enough to freeze spit.

"OK," said Mr Todd. "Time for the weather reports. Who wants to be our meteorologist for the day? Any predictions?"

Weather report from Antarctica: cloudy with a chance of never getting a Thomas Jefferson sticker.

The VIQ

On the way back to her seat, Jessica Finch
asked Judy, "How was Antarctica?"

"Long," said Judy.

What did Jessica Finch care anyway?
She probably knew how to spell *Antarctica*.
Even without sleeping on the dictionary.

Judy grumped. Judy slumped. Judy
Moody was down in the dumps. The
dumpiest. She, Madame M for Mistake,

could not predict the future – her own or anybody else's. She could not even predict one hour from now. Not one minute. Not one second. The future was *un-predictable*.

That did it. Judy decided then and there she would give up predicting the future. For ever. She had the Moody blues, the Judy-Moodiest.

She dragged herself to the water fountain at afternoon recess.

"Hel-lo? Judy? What is wrong with you?" asked Jessica Finch.

"I'm a flop. A big fat fake. I can't tell the future. Just call me Madame Phoney-Baloney."

"OK, Madame Phoney-Baloney!" said Jessica Finch. She laughed like a hyena. "If you say so. But I know something that tells the future. You can ask a question and it's N-E-V-E-R wrong."

Judy sprayed herself with water. How did Jessica Finch know so much about future-telling? "Really?"

"Really."

"Never?"

"Never!" said Jessica. "I'll bring it tomorrow. Think of something you want to ask. Something on your mind. Something that's been bugging you – a VIQ."

"VIQ?"

"Very Important Question," said Jessica.

Judy could hardly wait. She could hardly think about anything else. She could hardly sleep, even without the fat red dictionary under her pillow.

Judy thought and thought. She thought about something that had been on her mind. She thought about something that had been bugging her. She came up with a very important VIQ.

@ @ @

Judy got to school early Thursday morning. She rushed up to Jessica Finch. "Did you bring it? Did you?"

Jessica opened her pink plastic backpack and took out a bright yellow ball with a big smiley face on the outside. "Magic 8 Ball!" said Jessica.

"That's not a Magic 8 Ball," said Judy.

"Is too," said Jessica. "I'll show you."

"Will I always be the best speller at Virginia Dare School?" Jessica asked the Magic 8 Ball. The answer appeared in the window on a little triangle floating in blue liquid.

You're a winner.

"See? You try," said Jessica.

Judy decided to ask a practice question first. "Will my mood ring ever turn purple?" Judy shook the ball.

You look marvellous.

"Try again," said Jessica.

"Will my mood ring ever turn purple?"

Nice outfit.

"You're not asking right," said Jessica.

Judy shook the ball extra hard. "Will I be a doctor some day?"

Pure genius.

"Will I ever get a 110% Thomas Jefferson sticker on my spelling test?"

You're 100% fun.

"Will Mum and Dad be mad about my spelling test?"

Your breath is so minty!

"These aren't answers," said Judy. "Why is it saying all goopy stuff?"

"It's the Happy 8 Ball," said Jessica. "It only gives you good answers."

"No fair!" said Judy. "The Happy 8 Ball is a fake!"

"A good fake," said Jessica.

"I'm not going to ask my VIQ. I'll get a good answer, no matter what."

"Exactly," said Jessica.

"How can you believe what the Happy 8 Ball predicts if it just says goopy, good stuff all the time?" asked Judy.

"I don't care," said Jessica. "I like the Happy 8 Ball."

"I need an Un-happy 8 Ball!" said Judy.

"The one that doesn't lie."

And she knew just where to get it.

❀   ❀   ❀

Judy talked Rocky and Frank into going
with her to Vic's Mini-Mart after school.
Stink came too.

"I hope you're not getting a fake hand
to play another trick on me," said Stink.

"No," said Judy. "I'm getting a crystal
ball."

When they got to Vic's, Judy led them
all to the toy section. They saw troll doll
trading cards, an eyeball piggy bank and

some cat erasers. Then Judy spied one. A black ball with the real number 8 on it in a white circle.

"Magic 8 Ball!" said Judy. "The real one."

"That crystal ball is plastic," said Stink.

"It still tells the future," said Judy.

She held the Magic 8 Ball in the palm of her hand. She could almost feel its magic predicting powers.

"We can each ask one question," said Judy. "Who dares to ask the All-knowing Magic 8 Ball first?"

"Me, me, me!" said Frank.

"OK," said Judy, handing him the ball.

"Will I get a Jawbreaker Maker for my birthday?" asked Frank.

"You forgot to close your eyes tight and concentrate," said Judy.

Frank closed his eyes tight. Frank concentrated. He asked again. He shook the Magic 8 Ball. They all leaned over and peered into the tiny window.

Outlook not so good.

"I hope this thing lies," said Frank.

"Me next," said Rocky, taking the 8 Ball and shaking it. "Does Frank Pearl love Judy Moody?"

Signs point to yes.

"That's so funny I forgot to laugh," said Frank.

"Give me that," said Judy.

"My turn," said Stink.

"You only get one question, so think hard," Judy said. "And hurry up."

"Am I going to be president some day?" asked Stink.

Don't count on it.

"Will my little brother ever stop driving me crazy?" asked Judy.

Better not tell you now.

Stink grabbed the Magic 8 Ball back. "Does Rocky love Judy?"

"Do not anger the Magic 8 Ball," said the spooky-voiced Madame M. She peered into the little window. "Air bubble! See? You used up all your questions," Madame M pronounced. "We have to put it back now."

"How come?"

"Air bubble! It's the rules!"

Stink, Rocky and Frank went to buy gumballs.

"I'll catch up," Judy called.

Judy Moody did not put the Magic 8 Ball back on the shelf. She had one final question. The thing that had been bugging her for days. The VIQ.

Judy looked around. She concentrated. She shook the Magic 8 Ball. "Is Mr Todd in love?" Judy whispered.

Reply hazy, try again.

Judy closed her eyes. She held her breath. She said some magic words. "Eeny meany jelly beany," said Judy. "Is Mr Todd in love?"

She shook the Magic 8 Ball. She shook it some more. At last, she opened her eyes. There it was. The answer. In the window. A small triangle floating in blue liquid.

Yes, definitely.

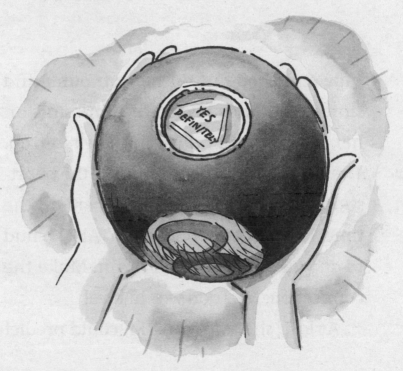

Operation True Love

Judy stretched out on her top bunk and stared up at the glow-in-the-dark stars on her ceiling. It all added up. The red ring. The new glasses, the humming, the heart-shaped cookies. It was right there all the time. Her best-ever prediction. All she had to do was see it. Use her brain. Make the connection. Mr Todd was in love!

At last, she, Madame M, could predict

something really, truly big. Something really, truly true. Something only she, Judy Moody, knew about. Judy had a new plan. A perfect, foolproof, fail-safe, predicts-the-future plan. All she had to do now was trick Mr Todd into trying on the mood ring. She had to see once and for all if it turned red for *Romantic, In Love*.

Only one thing stood in the way. She was not allowed to bring the mood ring to school.

👁 👁 👁

On Friday morning, Judy took out her mood ring. She did not wear it on her finger. She did not show it to anyone. She kept it hidden in her baby-tooth box.

She kept that hidden in the secret pocket of her backpack. Until the end of school.

Time for Project Mood Ring. Operation True Love. She, Doctor Judy Moody, was 3/4 sure and 9/10 certain that the Magic 8 Ball did not lie. But she had to be 110% sure-and-absolute positive.

"Mr Todd," said Judy, taking her mood ring out of the secret box. "I know I'm not supposed to bring my mood ring to school and everything, but I have a VIQ. A Very Important Question."

"I'm going to be in a bad mood if I see that ring in class again."

"I kept it put away all day," said Judy. "I promise. I was just hoping I could ask you how a mood ring works. In the name of science and everything."

"Mood rings *are* interesting," said Mr Todd. "They used to be popular when I was a kid, you know."

"No way!" said Judy.

"Way!" said Mr Todd, laughing. "Here, let me see that ring again."

Mr Todd held the ring with his fingers.

Judy tried to ESP Mr Todd a message. *Put the ring on. Put the ring on.*

"Mood rings have their own science."

Put the ring on.

"Did you know our bodies give off heat energy?"

Put the ring on.

Mr Todd slipped the ring onto the top of his index finger. "Liquid crystals change colour as our bodies change temperature. See? Red is for hot."

It worked! Red! The ring was R-E-D, *red*. Red for *Romantic*. Red for *In Love*. Red for sure and absolute positive.

"It is hot in here, isn't it?" said Mr Todd.

"*Red*-hot," said Judy. "Hot enough to melt Antarctica."

"I'm afraid Antarctica is here to stay," said Mr Todd. He handed her the ring. "Does that answer your Very Important Question?"

"Yes, yes, yes!" said Judy. "Thanks, Mr Todd!" Judy dashed out the door.

Madame M was back in business. And she was going to predict a future better than ever. Judy kissed her mood ring!

As soon as she reached the bus, she slipped it onto her finger. The ring turned amber. Amber meant *Nervous, Tense*. She knew what she was nervous about: her Judy Moody best-ever prediction. Before she could tell anybody, she had to figure out *who* Mr Todd was in love with. That was not going to be easy.

On Saturday morning, Judy went back to the library. She looked for Lynn, the friendly librarian with the fork-and-pie earrings.

Today, Lynn had skateboard earrings.

"You changed your earrings!" said Judy.

"I do that sometimes," said Lynn, and she laughed. "What can I help you with?"

"Where are the books that tell you if a person is in love?"

"Well, you know," Lynn said, "that kind of thing is hard to find in a book. Usually a person just sort of knows. Inside."

"Just so you know, it's not for me," Judy said, turning three shades of red. "I'm try-ing to figure out if someone else is in love."

"Ah. I see."

"You have a million gazillion books. There must be something in here with lovey-dovey stuff. Everybody likes love."

"Let me think a minute," said Lynn. "We do have Valentine's Day books. And love stories."

"No magic charms? Secret spells?"

"Let's try the 100s," Lynn said. She led Judy right to the love section and pulled a purple book with silver writing off the shelf. The silver writing said *Find Your True Love*. Judy opened it up and flipped through the pages. Chapter Five was titled "All You Need Is a Bowl of Molasses!"

"Molasses! That's easy! I'll take it!" said Judy. "Thanks!"

Judy read the book while she waited in line to check out. She read it as she walked home. She read it walking into her house.

In ancient times, staring into a bowl of molasses might reveal the identity of a true love.

Judy went straight to the kitchen and poured a jar of thick, sticky molasses into a bowl. She added some magic words. "Eeny meany chilli beany. Who does Mr Todd love?" She stared and stared into the molasses.

What she saw looked a little like ... a chicken.

No way! Mr Todd was not in love with a chicken.

Instead of molasses, people in Egypt looked into pools of ink.

Judy got a bottle of rubber-stamp ink from the desk in the hall. When she poured it into a bowl, all she saw was a big fat mess. And an ink splat on her shirt that looked like Antarctica. Nobody was in love with Antarctica.

Place a dish on a table and drop twenty-one safety pins into it.

She skipped that one. She did not have twenty-one pins, safe or unsafe.

Place a piece of wedding cake under your pillow and dream of the person you'll marry.

Wedding cake! Where on earth was she supposed to find wedding cake?

You will need a clock and a hairbrush.

Hairbrush? Judy had never met a hairbrush she liked. What did a hairbrush have to do with true love anyway? This love stuff sure was complicated!

Cut out twenty-six squares of paper, one for each letter of the alphabet. Place the letters of the alphabet face down in a bowl of water. The letters that turn face up will spell a loved one's name.

Bowl of water. Letters. She circled it. She could trick Mr Todd into that!

Press an apple seed to the forehead and recite the letters of the alphabet. When the seed falls off, that's the letter of the true love's name.

Apple seed. She could do that, too! She drew stars around that one.

Light a candle. If the wax drips to the left side, a woman is in love. Right side, a man is in love.

RARE!

Judy wrote a note to herself:

Non-Fiction Prediction

Judy was first to arrive in Room 3T on Monday morning.

"Judy, would you pass out crayons to everybody?" asked Mr Todd.

"What for?"

"Today we're going to do all our writing with crayons."

"What for?" Judy asked.

"For fun!"

"Magic Markers are better," said Judy.

Mr Todd frowned.

"I'm just saying."

"But don't you just love the smell of crayons?" asked Mr Todd.

Judy hurried up and passed out the not-Magic-Marker crayons. Then she asked Mr Crayon Smeller if she could conduct a scientific experiment on his desk.

She set a bowl of water with twenty-six paper letters next to his pencil jar.

She could hardly wait to see which letters turned right side up. Soon she, Madame M, would know the name of Mr Todd's secret love! She would no longer be Madame M for Mistake. No more Phoney-Baloney.

During Science class, Judy watched the letters float upside down in the bowl of water. Mr Todd was talking away about cumulus clouds. Judy drew puffy clouds with her Blizzard Blue crayon. She drew skinny clouds. She drew clouds shaped like hearts and crayons.

As soon as Science was over, Judy

rushed up to Mr Todd's desk. Lots of the upside-down paper squares had turned over! But all the Magic Marker letters had got runny and blurry in the water. She could not read one single letter!

"Did your experiment work?" asked Mr Todd.

"No," said Judy. "It came out a big fat zero."

"Try again," said Mr Todd. "True science takes time."

Yes, thought Judy. But this time she would use an apple seed.

❧　　❧　　❧

Judy ate the apple at lunch. At recess, she found Mr Todd in the playground talking with Rocky and Frank.

"Mr Todd," Judy asked, "will you help me with another experiment?"

"Anything for science," said Mr Todd.

"Put this apple seed on your forehead. Then say the alphabet."

"Fun-ny!" said Frank.

"Are you going to?" asked Rocky.

"Somehow this doesn't exactly sound scientific," said Mr Todd. He stuck the apple seed to his forehead. He started singing the alphabet song. "A B C D, E F G..." All the kids laughed.

"Is this a joke?" asked Mr Todd.

"Don't stop!" cried Judy. "You'll wreck the experiment!"

Mr Todd sang all the way to the letter *T* before the apple seed fell off.

The letter *T*, thought Judy. Hmm. Same as Todd.

"How'd I do?" asked Mr Todd.

"We'll see," said Judy. "True science takes time."

"Glad I could help. Now we'd better head back inside. Don't forget, today's the big day. Our special guest author is coming to visit 3T."

"You mean the Crayon Lady?" asked Frank. "Today?"

"How could you forget?" asked Judy. "Mr Todd's had crayons on the brain for a whole week."

Who cared about crayons anyway? Crayons were for kindergarteners. She had grown-up things to think about. Important things. Like L-O-V-E, *love*.

❧   ❧   ❧

Class 3T washed the blackboard and picked up scraps of paper under their chairs. They fed the fish and emptied the trash and erased pencil marks on their desks. Mr Todd wanted the room to look extra special, extra sparkling.

"We've never had to clean this much for anybody," said Frank.

"Tell me about it," said Judy. "Who's going to look in the trash anyway?"

"Her?" said Frank, pointing to a woman tapping on their door.

As soon as she came in, Class 3T put on

their best third-grade listening ears.

"Class 3T," said Mr Todd, "I would like you to meet a special friend of mine, Ms Tater. As you know, she's an author and an artist, and she's here today all the way from New York to tell us about the book she wrote called *Crayons Aren't for Eating*."

Everybody clapped. The Crayon Lady looked like a crayon! She wore a lemon-yellow top and a skirt like a painting. She had short, curly boy-hair and a fancy scarf around her head. She even had on crayon earrings. Best of all, she had melted orange crayon wax on her boots!

Ms Tater showed 3T her book about how crayons were made. She told the class it was *non-fiction*. *Non-fiction* meant the opposite of *fiction*. It meant true.

Ms Tater was non-old (young). She was non-ugly (pretty). And she was non-boring (interesting). She told the class how the first crayon was made a hundred years ago. She told about the secret formula for crayons, made of wax, colour and powder.

Then the author lit a candle and mixed the candle-wax drips with red powder to show how they make crayons. "It's like mixing flour in a cake mix," said Ms Tater.

Ms Tater told them how one time she met some famous guy named Captain Kangaroo at a crayon museum in New York. No lie.

She even told about the Crayon Eater machine. It was a big machine that checked for broken or lumpy crayons and threw the bad ones out.

Once, Ms Tater got to name her own crayon.

"What was it called?" everybody asked.

"Pumpkin Moon," she said, and she held up an orange crayon that matched her boots. "Mr Todd helped me think of it." Her smile was Night-light Bright.

"Some new names of crayons are Atomic Tangerine, Banana Mania and Eggplant."

Eggplant *was* a colour! Stink was right! "Is Zucchini a crayon?" asked Judy.

"No, but that's a good idea," said Ms

Tater. "And then there's my favourite: Purple Mountain Majesty."

"RARE!" said Judy. Purple Mountain Majesty! That was as good as Joyful, On-Top-of-the-World purple.

"Mr Todd's favourite is Vermilion."

"That's red," said Mr Todd.

Red! Judy sat up straight as a president and perked up her best third-grade listening ears.

"And we can't forget about Macaroni and Cheese!" Ms Tater held up a cheesy-looking crayon. "This one looks good enough to eat! But we'll leave that to the Crayon Eater machine." Everybody in Class 3T cracked up.

"Now it's your turn," Ms Tater said.

"Who can think up a good name for a crayon? Any ideas?"

"Baseball-mitt Brown!" said Frank.

"Piggy Pink!" said Jessica Finch.

"Mud," said Brad.

"Moody Blue!" said Judy.

When they were finished, Ms Tater let them ask questions.

"How long does it take to make a crayon?" asked Jessica Finch.

"About fifteen minutes."

"How long does it take to write a book?" asked Rocky.

"A lot longer than that. It took me about one year."

"Who invented crayons anyway? George Washington?" asked Frank.

"Well," said Ms Tater, "two guys named Binney and Smith made the first crayon. It was black. Mr Binney's wife, Alice, was a teacher, like Mr Todd. She invented the name Crayola."

"Any more questions?" asked Mr Todd.

Judy waved her hand in the air. "I have a comment, not a question."

"Yes?" said Ms Tater.

"You were so non-boring."

"Thank you," Ms Tater said. "What a great compliment."

Everybody clapped for the Crayon Lady when the programme was over.

"OK, 3T," said Mr Todd, "Ms Tater brought free crayons for all of us. Line up and I'll pass them out. Then you can go back to your seats and draw."

Judy got in line for her crayon. That's when she saw it. The candle! All the wax from the candle that Ms Tater lit had dripped to one side. The left side.

But wait! If Mr Todd was in love, the candle would have dripped to the *right* side. The left side meant a *woman* was in love.

Judy looked harder at the Crayon Lady. Mr Todd handed her a Vermilion Red crayon. Ms Tater smiled back at him like he had just turned into a handsome prince or something.

Or something! *Boing!* Of course! That was it! Ms Tater was in love! The candle drips proved it. Judy saw it with her own eyes. And *Tater* started with *T*. Just like the apple seed said.

At last, she, Judy Moody, had made a *non-fiction* prediction! Mr Todd was in love with the Crayon Lady! The Crayon Lady was in love with Mr Todd. There were a Vermilion and one reasons.

Purple Mountain Majesty

Judy Moody was in a tell-the-world mood. Judy told Frank Pearl. Judy told Rocky and Stink and the whole bus. Judy told Mum and Dad when she got home. She even called Jessica Finch. She announced to the whole world her best-ever, foretell-the-future, *non-fiction* prediction: "Madame M predicts ... twa-la! Mr Todd and the Crayon Lady are in love!"

By the next morning, Virginia Dare School was buzzing with the news. Really and truly? Could it be? Had Judy Moody predicted the future, once and for all? How did she know? Should they ask Mr Todd?

That morning, Class 3T sat about as still as popping popcorn.

"My, aren't we jumpy this morning," said Mr Todd.

"We have something we want to ask you," said Judy. She added three new bite marks to her pencil.

"Yes, yes, yes," everybody agreed.

"Well, before you ask me your question, I have some important news to tell all of you. It's a secret, but I think it's time I let you in on it."

Chomp, chomp. Judy chewed on her pencil eraser.

"You know Ms Tater, the author you met yesterday?"

Judy nearly choked on her pencil eraser! The whole class seemed to hold its breath. The popcorn stopped popping.

"I hope you enjoyed her presentation, and I hope you all learned something about making crayons and something about making books."

Bite, bite. Chomp.

"I told you Ms Tater is a special friend. And I'm so glad you all had a chance to meet her, because Ms Tater and I are engaged. We are going to be married! And you are all invited to our wedding."

"Wedding!" "Mmm, cake!" "Can I come?" "When?" "Will you still be our teacher?"

Questions and more questions zoomed around the room.

"Will there be a lot of crayons at your house?" asked Jessica Finch.

"Will your kids be the Tater-Todds?" asked Frank. He cracked himself up.

Judy did not even stop to laugh. "I KNEW IT!" She jumped right out of her seat. Her bite-mark pencil eraser flew to the front of the room. She practically did a dance right in the middle of the second row from the right.

"Judy Moody predicted it!" yelled Frank Pearl. "She was right!"

"She knew yesterday!" said Rocky. "She told us on the bus."

"She called me!" said Jessica Finch.

Everybody pointed to Judy. "She did! She told us! She knew! She predicted it right!"

"Judy," said Mr Todd, "is this true?"

"It's *non-fiction*," said Judy.

"How did you know? We thought we had a pretty good secret."

Judy thought of all the ways she knew. The mood ring turning red. The apple seed. The candle wax. But most of all it was the way Mr Todd smiled ear to ear around Ms Tater. And the way Ms Tater's eyes looked when she showed them the Pumpkin Moon crayon.

She could say it was the mood ring.

She could say it was ESP. She could say that she, Madame M for Moody, saw the future. Just like Jeane Dixon, Famous American Fortune-teller, without the eggs. But Judy realized – some things you just know. In your heart. There's no explaining them.

"How I knew is a secret," said Judy.

At last, she, Judy Moody, had predicted the future.

As soon as she got home, Judy ran straight to her room, opened up her extra-special baby-tooth box, and took out her mood ring. Judy slipped the mood ring onto her finger. She closed her eyes. She held her breath. She counted to eight, her favourite number. She thought of purple things: cool arm slings and dragonfly wings, grape bubblegum and not-pond-scum mood rings.

At last, Judy opened her eyes.

Black! The mood ring was black as Christmas-stocking coal. Black as a bad-luck ink splat. Black as a bad mood.

How could it be black when she was On-Top-of-Spaghetti happy? No, wait! The mood ring was changing. Yes. Right before her eyes. The mood ring turned purple! Mountain Majesty Purple! No lie. She, Judy Moody, was in a *Joyful, On-Top-of-the-World* mood.

Mr Todd said that everybody played a part in their own future, and the future was looking brighter already. From now on, Judy would take the future into her own hands, and there was no time like the present to get started.

She took out a non-Grouchy pencil and she wrote some non-fiction in her non-homework notebook.

Judy Moody's Plan for the Future

Become a Doctor doctor
Get stink to stop bothering me
Dress up for a fancy w
Dress up fancy for a wedding
Maybe write a book (not about crayons!)
Spell tortilla and zigzag the right way
Stay away from Antarctica
Paint my room Purple Mountain Majesty

The future was out there, waiting. And there was one more thing Judy did know for sure and absolute positive – there would be many more moods to come.

The *whole world's* in a Judy Moody mood!

Say hello to . . .

Fleur Humeur (Judy Moody in the Netherlands)

 or Dada Nalada (Judy Moody in Slovakia)

or Hania Humorek (Judy Moody in Poland).

The Judy Moody series has been published in more than twenty countries and languages, for a grand total of more than **12 million books** in print worldwide.

Open up a book – anywhere, any-time – and get ready for your *best mood ever*!

Have you read them all?

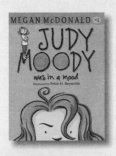

MEGAN McDONALD #1

JUDY MOODY

was in a mood

Illustrated by Peter H. Reynolds

MEGAN McDONALD #2

JUDY MOODY

Gets Famous!

Illustrated by Peter H. Reynolds

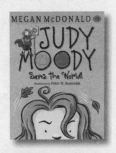

MEGAN McDONALD #3

JUDY MOODY

Saves the World!

Illustrated by Peter H. Reynolds

MEGAN McDONALD #4

JUDY MOODY

Predicts the Future

Illustrated by Peter H. Reynolds

MEGAN McDONALD #5

JUDY MOODY

The Doctor Is In!

Illustrated by Peter H. Reynolds

MEGAN McDONALD #6

JUDY MOODY

Declares Independence!

Illustrated by Peter H. Reynolds

MEGAN McDONALD #7

JUDY MOODY

Around the World in 8½ Days

Illustrated by Peter H. Reynolds

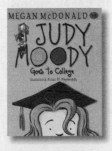

MEGAN McDONALD #8

JUDY MOODY

Goes to College

Illustrated by Peter H. Reynolds

MEGAN McDONALD #9

JUDY MOODY

Girl Detective

Illustrated by Peter H. Reynolds

Judy Moody's

Double-Rare
Way-Not-Boring
Book of
Fun Stuff to Do

Megan McDonald Illustrated by Peter H. Reynolds

Judy Moody's
Way Wacky
Uber Awesome
Book of
MORE Fun Stuff to Do

Megan McDonald Illustrated by Peter H. Reynolds

THE
Judy Moody
MOOD
JOURNAL

Megan McDonald
Illustrated by
Peter H. Reynolds

10 Things You May Not Know About Megan McDonald

10. The first story Megan ever got published (in the fifth grade) was about a pencil sharpener.

9. She read the biography of Virginia Dare so many times at her school library that the librarian had to ask her to give somebody else a chance.

8. She had to be a boring-old pilgrim every year for Halloween because she has four older sisters, who kept passing their pilgrim costumes down to her.

7. Her favourite board game is the Game of Life.

6. She is a member of the Ice-Cream-for-Life Club at Screamin' Mimi's in her hometown of Sebastopol, California.

5. She has a Band-Aid collection to rival Judy Moody's, including bacon-scented Band-Aids.

4. She owns a jawbreaker that is bigger than a baseball, which she will never, ever eat.

3. Like Stink, she had a pet newt that slipped down the drain when she was his age.

2. She often starts a book by scribbling on a napkin.

1. And the number-one thing you may not know about Megan McDonald is: she was once the opening act for the World's Biggest Cupcake!

10 Things You May Not Know About Peter H. Reynolds

10. He has a twin brother, Paul. Paul was born first, fourteen minutes before Peter decided to arrive.

9. Peter is part owner of a children's book and toy shop called the Blue Bunny in the Massachusetts town where he lives.

8. He's vertically challenged (aka short!).

7. His mother is from England; his father is from Argentina.

6. He made his first animated film while he was in high school.

5. He sometimes paints with tea instead of water – whatever's handy!

4. He keeps a sketch pad and pen on his nightstand. That way, if an idea hits him in the middle of the night, he can jot it down immediately.

3. His favourite candy is a tie between peanut-butter cups and chocolate-covered raisins (same as Megan McDonald!).

2. One of his favourite books growing up was *The Tall Book of Make-Believe* by Jane Werner, illustrated by Garth Williams.

1. And the number-one thing you may not know about Peter H. Reynolds is: he shares a birthday with James Madison, Stink's favourite president!

DOUBLE RARE!
Judy Moody has her own interactive website!

Visit **www.judymoody.com** for all things
Judy Moody and lots of way-not-boring
fun stuff, including:

- ✪ The Official Judy Moody Fan Club

- ✪ Interactive games and a Mood Meter

- ✪ Way-not-boring stuff about Megan McDonald
  and Peter H. Reynolds

- ✪ Digital downloads, including emoticons and
  wallpapers

- ✪ Sample chapters and downloadable reading logs

Be sure to check out Stink's adventures too!

Judy and Stink are starring together!

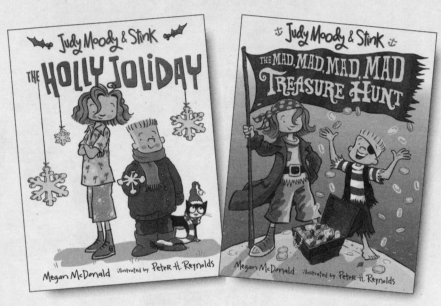

Judy Moody and Stink
The Holly Joliday

Judy Moody and Stink
The Mad, Mad, Mad, Mad
Treasure Hunt

In full colour!